W9-BYK-752

A SELFIE -01

STEP 2: ALERT SYSTEM ON ROOF

STEP 4 : CAPTURE SANTA

FREDDY MELCHER
OFFICIAL BLUEPRINT OF MELCHER INC.

The Great Santa Stakeout

written by **BETSY BIRD**

illustrated by **DAN SANTAT**

ARTHUR A. LEVINE BOOKS

AN IMPRINT OF SCHOLASTIC INC.

For Jack Bird, one smart, slick spy guy —BB

For Alek and Kyle —DS

Text copyright © 2019 by Betsy Bird
Illustrations copyright © 2019 by Dan Santat

All rights reserved.
Published by Arthur A. Levine Books,
an imprint of Scholastic Inc., *Publishers since 1920*.
SCHOLASTIC and the LANTERN LOGO are trademarks
and/or registered trademarks of Scholastic Inc.

The publisher does not have any control over and does not assume any responsibility for author or third-party websites or their content.

No part of this publication may be reproduced, stored in a retrieval system, or transmitted in any form or by any means, electronic, mechanical, photocopying, recording, or otherwise, without written permission of the publisher. For information regarding permission, write to Scholastic Inc., Attention: Permissions Department, 557 Broadway, New York, NY 10012.

This book is a work of fiction. Names, characters, places, and incidents are either the product of the author's imagination or are used fictitiously, and any resemblance to actual persons, living or dead, business establishments, events, or locales is entirely coincidental.

LIBRARY OF CONGRESS CATALOGING-IN-PUBLICATION DATA AVAILABLE

ISBN 978-1-338-16998-0

10 9 8 7 6 5 4 3 2 1 19 20 21 22 23

Printed in Malaysia 108
First edition, September 2019

The text type was set in Futura Bold and Victorian Std.
The display type was set in Victorian Std.
The illustrations were created with ink, watercolor, and Adobe Photoshop.

Art direction and book design by Marijka Kostiw

Freddy Melcher was Santa's #1 Fan.

He was the kind of kid who'd dress up as Santa for birthday parties . . .

HAPPY

and Valentine's Day . . .

and even Talk Like a Pirate Day.

BUS
STOP

I KNOW WHEN YOU ARE SLEEPING
HO-HO HOTEL
NO VACANCY
SHAVE
25¢
NORTH POLE
SANTA CLAUS LN
Santa Claus
ACTION FIGURE
KRIS KRINGLE
64 POINTS OF ARTICULATION
SANTA
REINDEER FUD

Freddy had **Santa** posters, **Santa** action figures, and **Santa** underwear. He was even saving up to buy his own pet reindeer. But there was one prize Freddy desperately wanted: a photograph taken *with* **Santa**, fresh out of the chimney.

Oh, it was risky. As every good kid knows, Santa only visits when everyone's in bed. It's awfully hard to sneak anything by someone who can see you when you're sleeping and knows when you're awake.

That's why Freddy had to be extra good this year . . . at hiding his plans.

ANTA SELFIE - 01
CANS FOR REINDEER ARRIVAL
CAMERA
DDY MELCHER
AL DOCUMENT OF MELCHER INC.

STEP 1 in Freddy's plan: String the roof with cans, so the sleigh can't land undetected.

STEP 2: Rig the whole living room with motion-sensitive cameras.

STEP 3: **Put the milk and cookies on a pressure-sensitive plate.**

STEP 4: Practice staying up late.

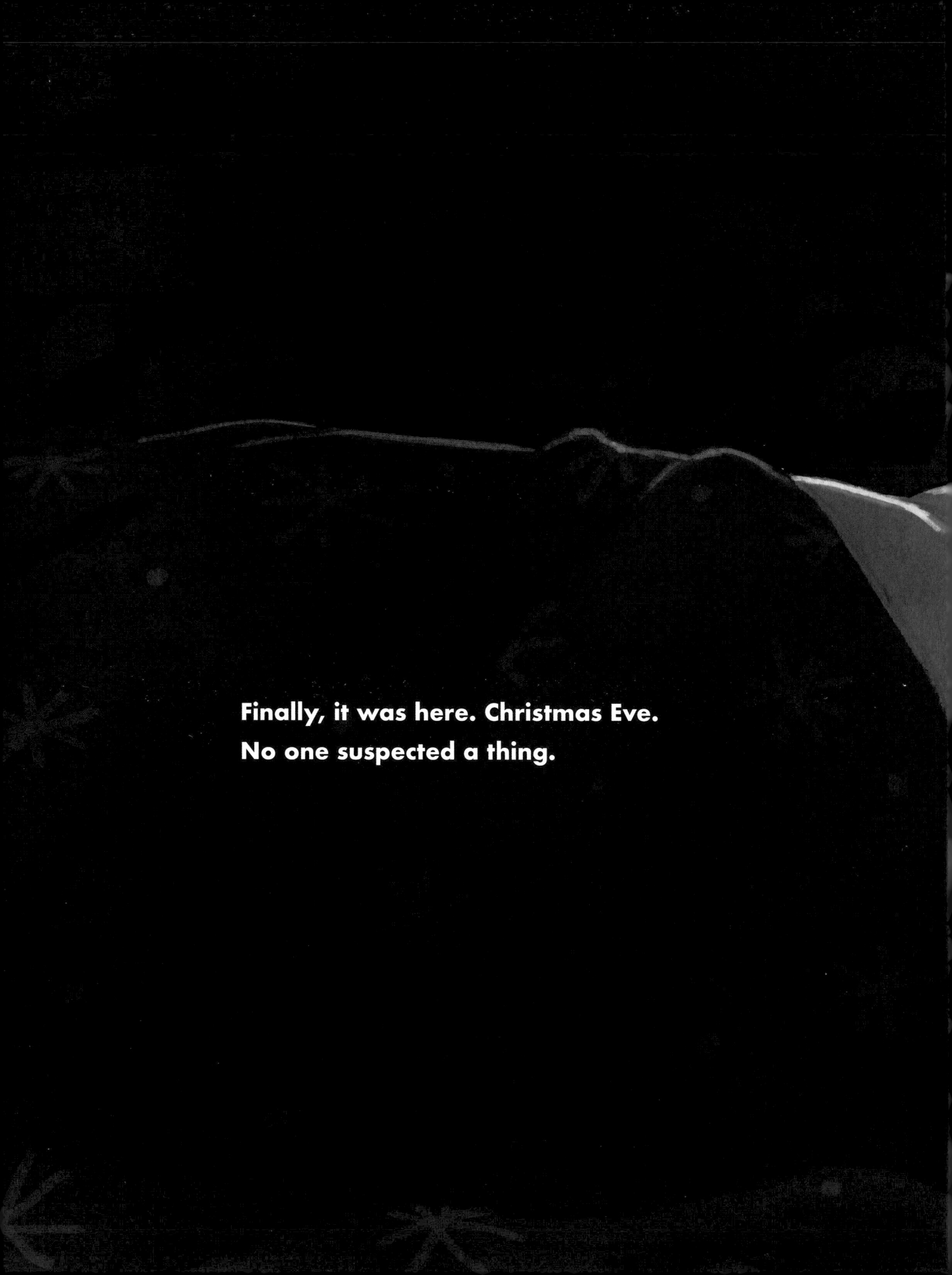

Finally, it was here. Christmas Eve.
No one suspected a thing.

SANTA
HO HO HO

Freddy was vigilant. It was almost midnight, and Santa should be here any second, yeah . . . any . . . any . . .

zzzzzzzzzzz...

SOOP

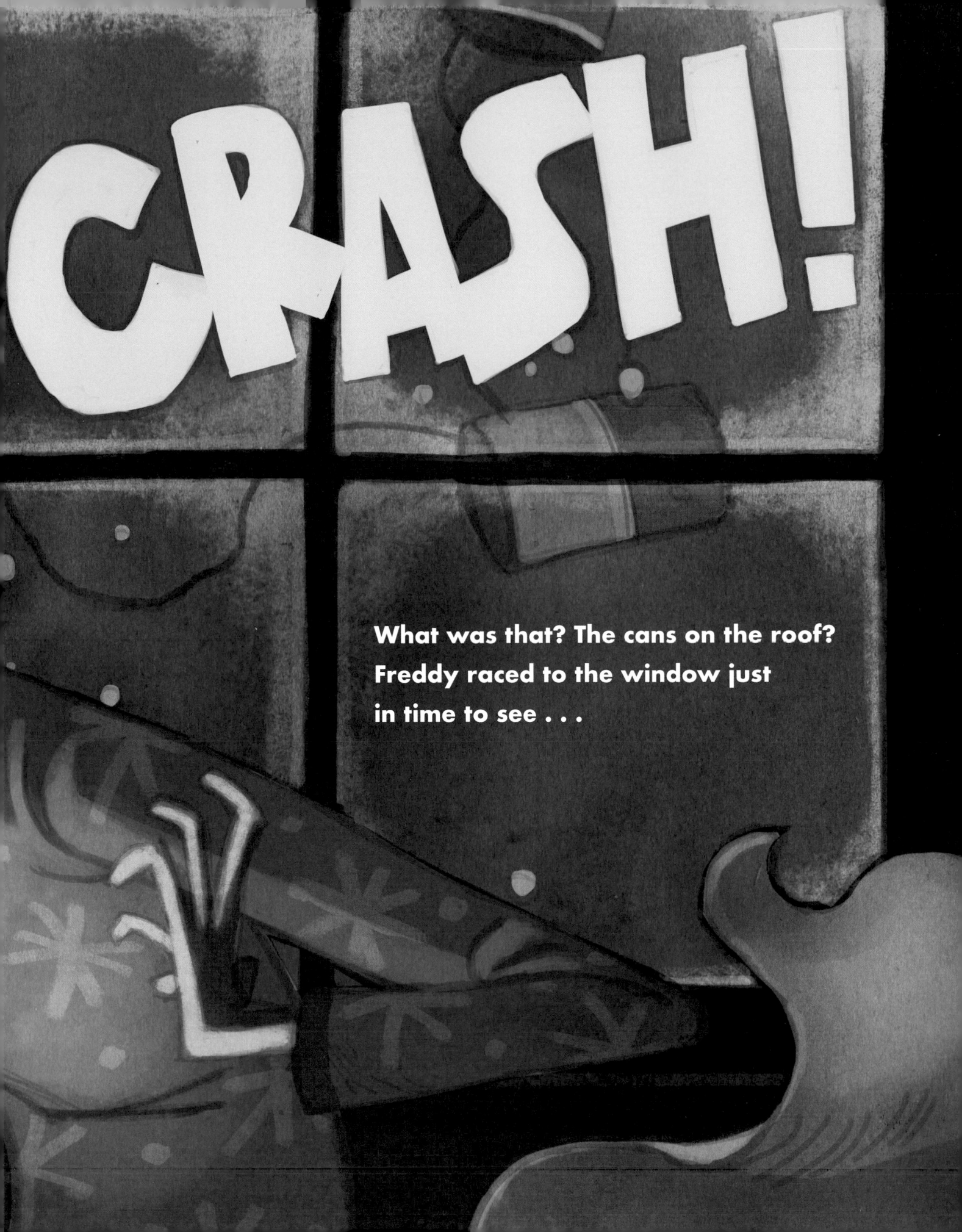

What was that? The cans on the roof? Freddy raced to the window just in time to see . . .

DISASTER!

Something big rolled right off the roof.

Freddy tore outside. What had he done?

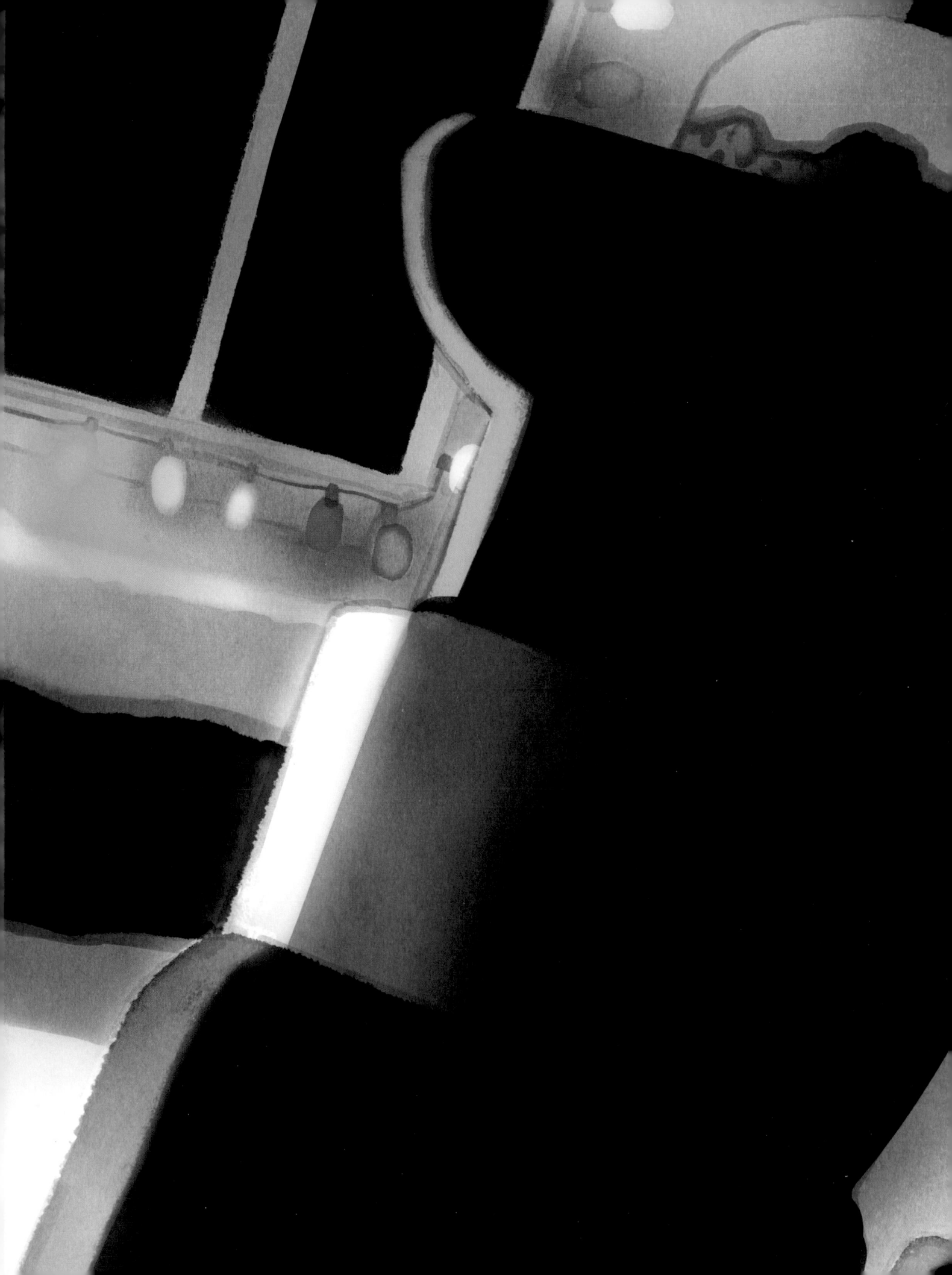

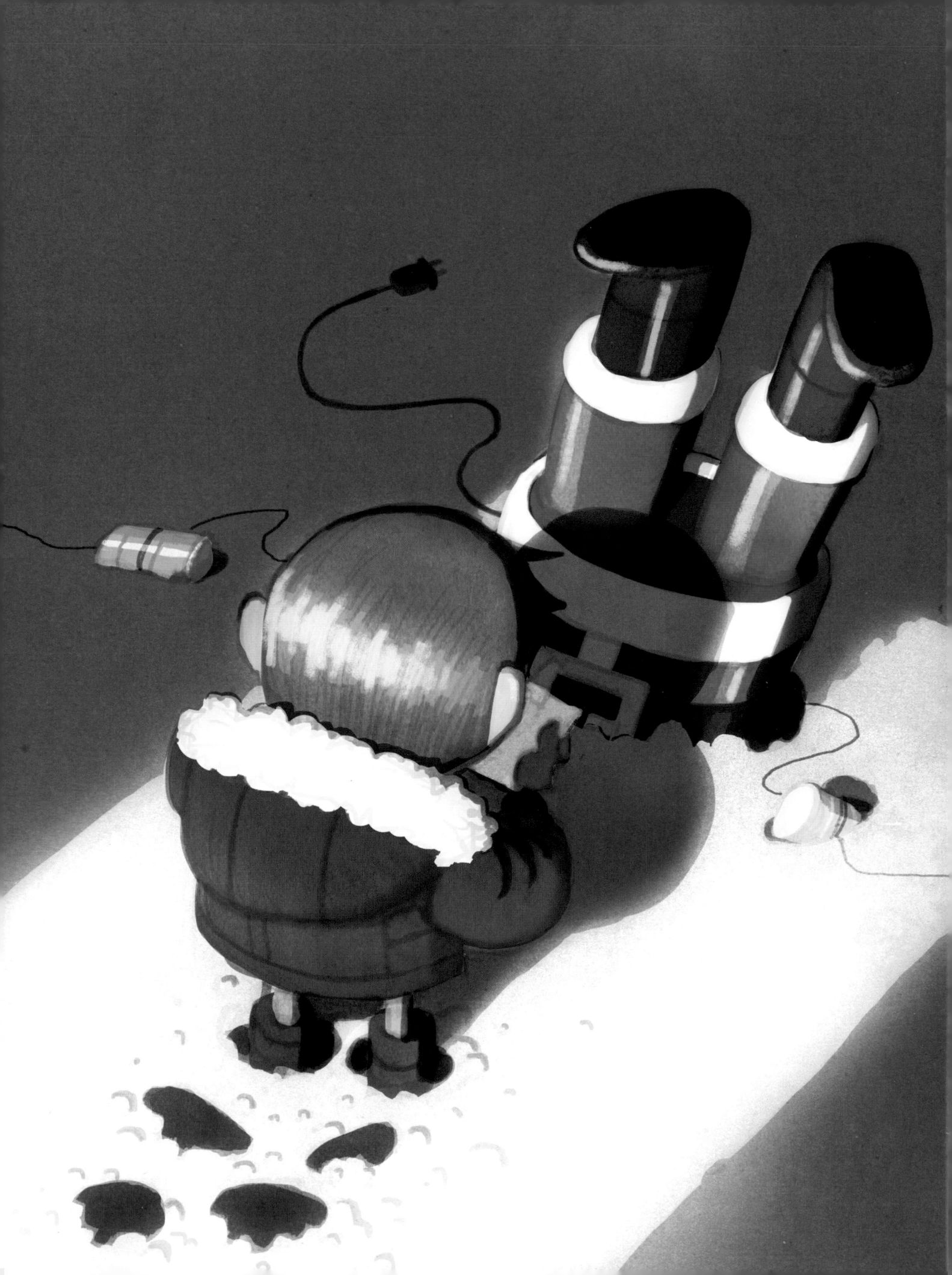

Santa had duped him and dashed!

Freddy was . . . angry?
No, that's not it.

Embarrassed?
No, no. Not that either.

He was sobbing his heart out,
pounding the snow,
having the most broken tantrum
of his short life?
Well, actually Freddy felt . . .

FANTASTIC.

While other kids nestled all snug in their beds, Freddy had played hide-and-seek with his hero! He even had a note from Santa that he could add to his collection.

So what if Santa got away this year?
It's fine. Maybe it's for the best.
Maybe no one can outwit Santa Claus . . .

no one, that is, except Freddy.
Hey. There's always next year!

NTA SELFIE -02
STEP 2:
BOX FALLS
ON SANTA
OH NO!
I CAN'T SEE
THE COOKIES!
STEP 3:
TAKE SELFIE
WITH SANTA
YAY! YOU
ARE SO
SMART!
HAVE A
COOKIE!
REDD
SANTA CLAUS
NORTH POLE
NICE TRY,
FREDDY!
-SANTA

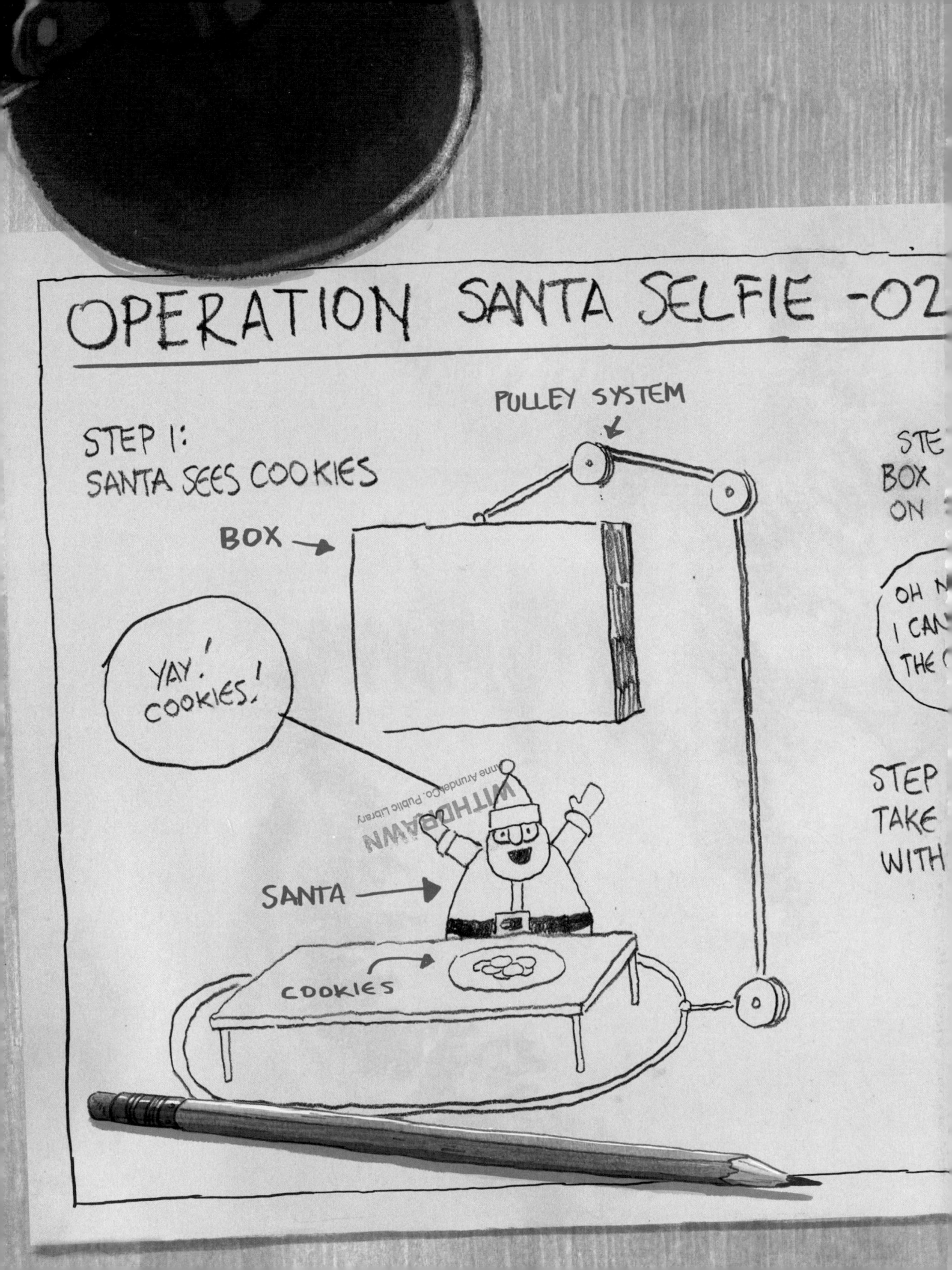

WITHDRAWN
Anne Arundel Co. Public Library